Dedications

Kay Northam—Wonderful friend, always there, always helpful, using her time unsparingly to assist me. Kay helped to shape my presentations and did all my typing.

Doyle Shivers—Son, my steadfast rock. His unshakable faith never faltered nor wavered.

Rosanne Burgess—Librarian, a true helper. All resources were at my disposal. She called *Twinkle Star & Mother Moon* a real classic—universal in appeal and not set in any time frame— good yesterday, good today, and good tomorrow.

—*L. J. W.*

Twinkle Star and Mother Moon

Enchanted Rock
An imprint of Gulf Publishing Company
Book Division
P.O. Box 2608 □ Houston, Texas 77252-2608

10 9 8 7 6 5 4 3 2 1

Library of Congress Cataloging-in-Publication Data

Watkins, Leola.
   Twinkle Star and Mother Moon / Leola Watkins ; illustrated by Charmayne Thevenet.
     p. cm.
   Summary: A mischievous little star disobeys Mother Moon and almost ends up sliding right out of heaven.
   ISBN 0-88415-235-9 (alk. paper)
   [1. Stars Fiction. 2. Moon Fiction. 3. Behavior Fiction.] I. Thevenet, Charmayne, ill. II. Title.
PZ7.W274Tw   1999
[E]—dc21
                                            99-34283
                                          CIP

Printed in Hong Kong.

Printed on acid-free paper (∞).

Art direction/book and cover design by Roxann L. Combs.

Once there was a little star.
He lived up in the blue, blue heavens.
This little star was called Twinkle Star.
In the daytime, Twinkle Star and all
the other little stars were fast asleep
behind the rays of the sun.

But at night, when the sky turned midnight blue, Mother Moon called all her little stars to her and put them, one by one, in their places on little, red sky hooks. Each star made a tiny bright light, and this light could be seen all the way down to Earth.

*N*ow when Mother Moon put each star in a certain place for the night, that little star stayed right there until morning. That is, all of them but one. Twinkle Star.

Twinkle Star liked to play and tease Mother Moon and the other little stars, too. Twinkle would slip off his hook, dash behind another star, and call, "Peek-a-boo." This was not the proper way for a little star to behave, so Mother Moon called him and put him back in his place each time. But Twinkle could not stay still.

One evening, as the daytime sky was turning into the nighttime sky, Mother Moon called all her little stars together, just as she always did, and put them, one by one, in their places.

"Now Twinkle," Mother Moon said right before she placed him in the sky, "I want you to be a good little star tonight and stay in your place. Will you do that for your Mother Moon? I'm going to be busy with the harvest."

"Yes, Mother Moon," answered Twinkle Star. "I will be good tonight and stay in my place."

*T*winkle Star was a truthful little star, and he honestly meant to stay in his place that night, as he promised Mother Moon. But soon he forgot all about his promise, slipped off his hook, and went running around in the heavens, hiding behind the other stars and playing peek-a-boo as usual.

Mother Moon was so busy sending her moonbeams down to Earth for light that she didn't see Twinkle Star.

Suddenly Twinkle Star noticed the Milky Way stretching across the sky. A thought popped into his mind. A thought about the Milky Way that was new. "My, what a nice slide that Milky Way would make."

He moved closer and closer to the Milky Way. Sliding on it would be a daring trick, and Twinkle was a little afraid to try.

"*I*'m going to do it!" Twinkle exclaimed. "I can jump off before I reach the end. What fun I will have!" So Twinkle Star hurried to the very top of the Milky Way. He climbed up on it and took a deep breath.

He turned loose. Whe-e-e-ee! Such fun! Twinkle was sliding down the Milky Way.

"Look at me! Look at me!" Twinkle called as he whizzed by the other stars. He was going faster and faster. Oh, this was fun.

"Now is the time to jump," Twinkle thought. "Right now before I slide out of heaven."

But Twinkle Star was sliding so fast that he could not jump! All he could do was sit and slide!

Just then he reached the end of the Milky Way, and he shot right off. Twinkle Star became a shooting star, hurtling through the heavens.

"Oh, my!" Twinkle cried. "What can I do?"

He knew shooting stars shot straight out of heaven and fell to Earth and that was the end of them.

He began clutching at everything he passed, but he was falling too fast to hold on.

"Mother Moon, Mother Moon! Oh, please help me!" Twinkle begged. "Oh, please help me."

Mother Moon turned and saw that Twinkle Star was in trouble.

"Oh, Twinkle!" she exclaimed, and quick as a
comet flash she wrapped a moonbeam around
Twinkle and pulled him back into heaven.
"Thank you, Mother Moon. Thank you," he said.

*T*hen he remembered his promise to Mother Moon. He had promised her that he would stay in his place, but he had forgotten. And he had almost been lost for good. He sighed. But Mother Moon didn't say a word. She didn't scold Twinkle Star at all.

*J*ust then, Twinkle spied the tall sky ladder.

He marched through the moon dust toward the sky

ladder and climbed to the tip-top of it.

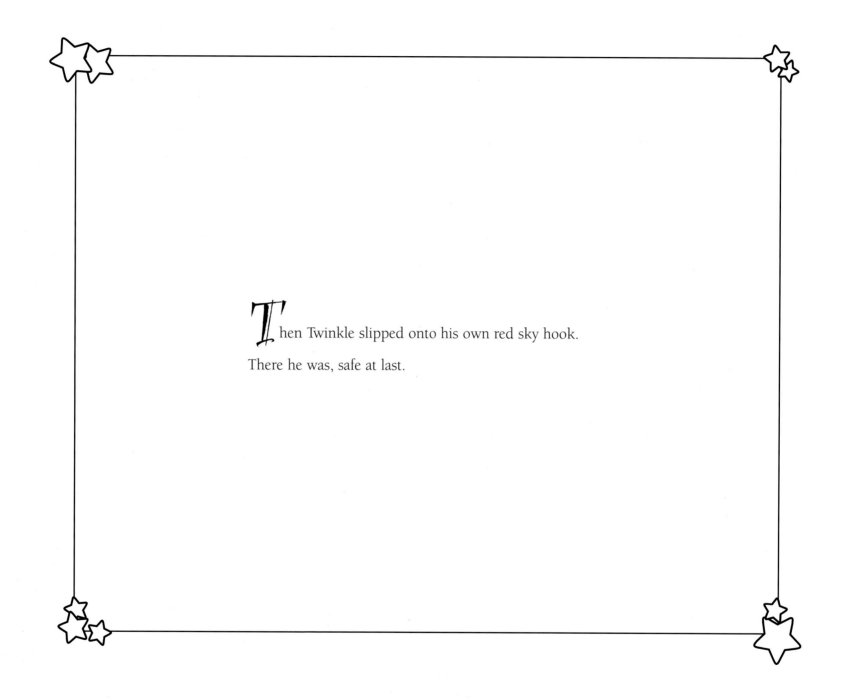

*T*hen Twinkle slipped onto his own red sky hook.

There he was, safe at last.

"Promises are made for keeping," Twinkle Star thought, as he happily dangled under the watchful eye of Mother Moon.

Bright Points about Astronomy

🌠 The North Star, Polaris, is the only star that doesn't rise and set. That's why sailors can find their way by using it; it's always in its place.

🌠 The harvest moon comes in September and is the closest full moon of the year.

🌠 A star's color is determined at birth. The more mass the star has, the hotter it is. Hotter stars are white, while smaller, cooler stars have a red color.

🌠 If you were to stand on the crescent moon to look at the Earth, the Earth would appear as a crescent.

🌠 Every star that can be seen with the naked eye is within the Milky Way.

🌠 On July 22, 1995, two amateur astronomers in two different states discovered a previously unknown comet in the heavens. It would be named after the two astronomers: Alan Hale from New Mexico and Tom Bopp from Arizona. Both regularly watched the sky, but Tom Bopp did not even own a telescope. He borrowed a friend's telescope to do his observations. Comet Hale-Bopp is thought to be the most important comet of the 20th century.

For links to websites containing more fun astronomy facts, visit
WWW.ENCHANTEDBOOKS.com